Princess Poppy
Happy Ever After

written by Janey Louise Jones
Illustrated by Samantha Chaffey

HAPPY EVER AFTER

A YOUNG CORGI BOOK 978 0 552 56658 2

Published in Great Britain by Young Corgi,
an imprint of Random House Children's Publishers UK
A Random House Group Company

This edition published 2009

Text copyright © Janey Louise Jones, 2009
Illustrations copyright ©Random House Children's Publishers UK, 2009
Illustrated by Samantha Chaffey

The Random House Group Limited supports The Forest Stewardship Council
(FSC®), the leading international forest certification organisation. Our books
carrying the FSC label are printed on FSC® certified paper. FSC is the only
forest certification scheme endorsed by the leading environmental organisations,
including Greenpeace. Our paper procurement policy can be found at
www.randomhouse.co.uk/environment

MIX
Paper from
responsible sources
FSC   FSC® C016897
www.fsc.org

Young Corgi Books are published by Random House Children's Publishers UK,
2009 Illustrated by Samantha Chaffey, 61–63 Uxbridge Road, London W5 5SA

www.princesspoppy.com

www.randomhouse.co.uk

Addresses for companies within The Random House Group Limited can be
found at: www.randomhouse.co.uk/offices.htm

THE RANDOM HOUSE GROUP Limited Reg. No. 954009

A CIP catalogue record for this book is available from the British Library.

Printed and bound by CPI Group (UK) Ltd, Croydon, CR0 4YY

Princess Poppy
Happy Ever After

Check out Princess Poppy's website
to find out all about the other
books in the series
www.princesspoppy.com

For all those who believe in happy endings

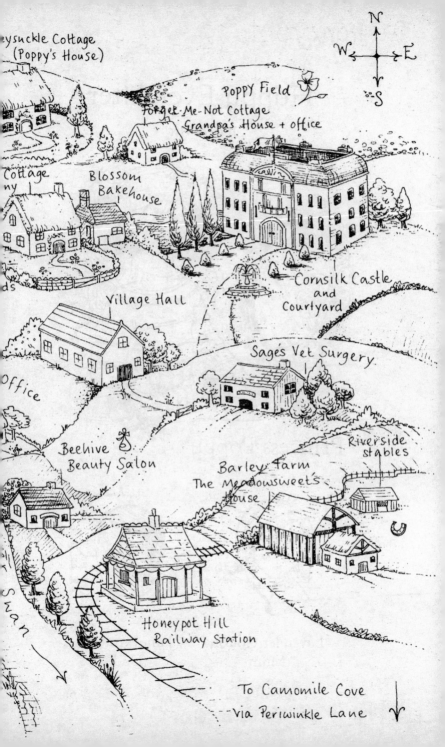

Happy Ever After

featuring

Princess Poppy

Lavender Cotton
(Mum)

James Cotton
(Dad)

Granny Bumble   Honey   Sweetpea

Mimosa   Abigail   Sally Meadowsweet

Sol Melville   Farmer Meadowsweet   Saffron Sage

Chapter One

Poppy was very excited. She had just received an invitation to her first ever barn dance. It was to be at Barley Farm the following Friday, and the theme was country and western. She raced over to see Honey right away to talk about their outfits, and with a little help from Granny Bumble they had soon both decided on red and white gingham dresses and cowboy hats.

On the day of the dance Poppy dressed with great care and turned to admire herself in her bedroom mirror. She particularly loved the fringed cowboy boots that Mum had found in a charity shop, and her big Stetson hat.

"Yee-haa!" she said to herself as she did
another turn in front of the mirror.

"Come on, Poppy," called Mum. "You *must*
be ready by now! We're going to miss Farmer
Meadowsweet on the bucking bronco if we don't
go now!"

"Just coming, Mum," replied Poppy as she
grabbed her things and ran down to meet the
rest of her family.

"I'm going to try that bucking bronco too!" said Dad. "I bet I can stay on the longest!"

"Well, make sure you don't hurt yourself!" scolded Mum. "Right, let's go then."

Dad took Poppy's hand and they giggled together as they made their way down to Barley Farm with Mum walking beside them.

"Remember we can't be late home," she told them. "Grandpa can only babysit the twins until nine. And, James, don't drink too much punch – it's really potent, apparently."

"Yes, dear!" replied Dad, rolling his eyes and winking at Poppy.

Sometimes Mum was no fun at all.

When they arrived at the farm Poppy could hardly believe her eyes. Farmer and Mrs Meadowsweet had gone to so much effort – it looked just like a scene from one of the old cowboy films that Grandpa liked to watch. There was a huge tent set up next to the big barn, and colourful banners and bunting garlanded the farmyard. There were games

and stalls and a band playing fiddle music in the barn. A vast barbecue grill was smoking away near the tent, with tables set out all around it, laden with crisp salads, spicy sauces, crusty bread and fat herb sausages, and the air was filled with the most delicious cooking smells.

"Hi, cowgirls!" said Poppy as she ran to greet Honey, Sweetpea and Mimosa, who were all standing together near the entrance to the barn. "This is so cool! You all look amazing! Where's Abi?"

"Oh, she's got a violin exam tomorrow so her mum and dad said that she had to practise tonight," explained Sweetpea.

"Oh, shame, she would love this," said Poppy.

"Let's go and look at the bucking bronco," suggested Mimosa.

"Ooo, yeah, let's," said Honey.

"Come on, then," replied Poppy. "Follow me!"

The four friends made their way to the meadow, where the crazy rodeo-style "bull" was in action. Farmer Meadowsweet was holding on for dear life and looking very red in the face. Mum had been right – this was definitely too good to miss. He looked so funny. As they stood there watching, Cousin Saffron's husband, David, came over and told them that the farmer has been practising on it all week because he wanted to be able to stay on for two whole minutes.

Poor Farmer Meadowsweet looked as though his arms were about to fall off – this seemed like the longest two minutes ever.

"Just let go, you silly old fool!" called Mrs Meadowsweet. "Sally, you tell your father to stop – he's going to have one of his bad turns."

Sally Meadowsweet didn't look at all worried; there was no way she could have said anything to her father – she was laughing so much she couldn't get a single word out!

"Quick! Someone do something!" wailed Mrs Meadowsweet. "This is not good for a man of his age!"

But just then, the farmer let go of the bull and tumbled off onto the hay below in a crumpled heap.

"I told you I could do two minutes, didn't I?" he chuckled, exhausted. "Now, who's going to help an old man up?"

Sally's boyfriend, Sol, who was a doctor in Strawberry Corner, rushed over to help the farmer up and check that he was OK.

"I think he'll live, but he'll need a glass of punch to revive him!" Sol announced to the guests, and a big cheer went up.

"Now, he's the sort of doctor we need round here," said Farmer Meadowsweet merrily.

Poppy's dad was next up on the bucking bronco. He whispered to Poppy that he was going to better Farmer Meadowsweet's record by staying on for a full three minutes.

Poppy watched nervously as her dad clung onto the bull and was very proud indeed when he broke the record. He could hardly walk afterwards but luckily Mum didn't notice as she was busy throwing hoops onto a cone, trying to win teddies for the twins. Poppy knew what

Mum would have said if she had seen Dad hobbling around: "Told you so!"

"Well, I think I deserve some of that punch now – don't tell your mother, Poppy!" Dad smiled. "I'll see you girls later."

Poppy, Honey, Mimosa and Sweetpea decided that it was time to try some line dancing so they headed over to the big barn. The steps

were being called out by Len, the lead singer of The Cattlemen. All the villagers were having a wonderful time stepping to the beat, with calls of "Yee-haa!" every now and then! The girls joined in immediately and soon got the hang of it.

After a while Mum came over to say that it was time to go home, but just then Poppy noticed Farmer Meadowsweet climbing up onto the hay-bale stage and walking over to the microphone.

"Please can we stay, Mum – just to hear what he's going to say?" she begged.

"Someone's got to get back for the twins

but I suppose it doesn't need to be all of us. I'll go and you and Dad can stay," agreed Mum.

"Thank you, Mum!"

Poppy and Dad kissed Mum goodbye and turned back to look at the stage.

"It is wonderful to see so many of you here tonight," began the farmer. "This barn dance is just our way of saying thank you to everyone for buying local produce and keeping us in business! Well, that is one of the reasons for the party. The other reason – and the most important one, I think – is to share some very special news with you. My beautiful daughter Sally is getting married to Sol Melville. Mrs Meadowsweet and I cannot wait for him to officially be part of the family – the son we never had. I mean, Dr Sol

Meadowsweet sounds good, doesn't it?" he joked.

There was a huge cheer and lots of laughing and shouts of "Congratulations!" and "About time too, Sal!"

Poppy was thrilled at the news – she simply adored weddings.

Chapter Two

The next day, desperate to hear all about Sally's
wedding plans, Poppy and Honey headed over
to the Lavender Valley Garden Centre. When
they arrived they found Sally and Sol sitting
on a bench in the lavender garden. They were
chatting happily about the party the previous
night and discussing plans for their wedding,
such as where to exchange their vows and
which date to pick.

"Hello, girls!" called Sally. "What brings
you here?"

"We wanted to see your ring!" replied Poppy.
"Please will you show us?"

They hadn't managed to get a look the night before – Sally had been surrounded by people after the announcement.

Sally held out her left hand proudly.

"Wow!" gasped Honey.

"It's so sparkly!" said Poppy. "I love it!"

"Me too," laughed Sally.

"When's the wedding going to be?" asked Honey breathlessly.

"Well, we think we've decided on a date, don't we, darling?" said Sol.

"Yes, we certainly have. It'll be in two months' time, Honey, at the end of the summer," Sally told them. "We can't wait!"

"And where will it be?" asked Honey.

"We're not sure yet," replied Sally.

"Do you have a theme?" Poppy wondered.

"Um, gosh, we haven't really thought about that sort of thing. I think you girls might know more about planning a wedding that we do!" said Sally, sounding a little flustered. "There certainly seems to be a lot to think about, and not much time. Oh dear, I do hope everything will run smoothly."

"Don't you worry, my darling," said Sol, putting his arm around his fiancée. "I just know that our day will be wonderful, whatever happens."

Sally smiled back at him.

Just then Farmer and Mrs Meadowsweet arrived on their tractor. They were delivering some fertilizer for Sally's flowers and had also come to talk about wedding plans.

"Can you believe that man – making me come through the village in my nice frock on that stinking muck machine?" complained Mrs Meadowsweet.

"This is a very fine machine, I'll have you know!" replied Farmer Meadowsweet indignantly. "And when did you get so la-di-dah?"

"Oh dear, is this what I've got to look forward to when we're married?" whispered Sol to Sally. "They do say we all get more and more like our parents as we get older!"

"Don't be mean," giggled Sally, giving him a playful slap. "We'll never be like that, I promise."

"I'm not deaf, you know," said Mrs Meadowsweet. "Honestly, we give you a tip-top barn dance and this is the way you talk about us! Now, how about telling us where you've got to with the wedding plans."

"We have to go home now or we'll be late for lunch," Poppy said to Sally. "Thank you for showing us your ring. We would really like to help with wedding stuff – if you want us to, that is. Me and Honey are very good at organizing and making things, aren't we?"

Honey nodded her agreement.

"Oh, thank you, girls. You are sweet," said Sally.

"Aren't weddings just so cool, Honey?" sighed Poppy as they walked back towards their homes. "I think Sally and Sol are just like a fairytale prince and princess."

"Yeah, they are. I can't wait to see them on their wedding day," agreed Honey. "But all that kissing and cuddling is a bit gross. When my mum and dad get all smoochy like that, I get really embarrassed, don't you?"

"I suppose so," replied Poppy. "Although actually my mum and dad don't really do that stuff – not any more anyway."

She said goodbye to Honey and walked up the garden path to her front door. She arrived in the kitchen to find Dad heating up soup for lunch. Mum was on the phone, taking a hat order for Sally's wedding.

"Hello, darling," said Dad. "Almost time for lunch."

While Poppy was waiting, she decided to have a look at Mum and Dad's wedding album. She hadn't looked at it for ages, and all the wedding chat had reminded her how much she loved their photos. She went into the sitting room and opened the cupboard where Mum kept all the family photographs in special albums. Her parents' wedding album had a lovely satin cover and was tied with pretty

ribbons. Poppy flipped
the album open. She
couldn't take her
eyes off the beautiful
shots of Mum and
Dad. They looked so
young and happy.
In every picture
they were laughing or
cuddling or smiling at
each other, very much
like Sally and Sol were
behaving at the moment.
Mum's dress was amazing,
all lacy and delicate, and
she wore a pretty floral
headdress too. Dad
was wearing a dark
suit, crisp white shirt and
lilac tie and he looked very
handsome – he had a lot
more hair then!

Mum hardly ever put on dresses or looked glamorous nowadays. Ever since the twins had been born she wore boring, sensible clothes and no make-up. She said it was because they were forever spilling things on her – and anyway, she had no time to think about herself any more.

Just then Poppy noticed the date on the album.

Wow! It will be their tenth anniversary two weeks before Sally's wedding! That's a LONG time! she thought.

Poppy was absolutely fascinated by the wedding pictures. It was lovely to see Granny Mellow looking so pretty, although it made Poppy a bit sad to think that she had never known her mum's mum.

And Saffron was such a beautiful bridesmaid, her long copper hair decorated with fresh garden flowers. Poppy found it amazing and weird to imagine her parents' life before she was born – looking at their wedding photos always made her think about it though.

"Lunch is ready," called Dad, interrupting Poppy's thoughts.

She put away the album and went to wash her hands.

During lunch, Mum took charge of feeding the twins and she and Dad discussed their plans for the rest of the weekend.

"I've got a lot of hats to get started on so if you could take the children to the adventure playground, James, that would be great," said Mum. "Oh, and we'll need to get the house cleaned and the ironing done at some point too."

"Right-o," replied Dad. "So much for relaxing over the weekend."

"As for tomorrow, Grandpa, Granny Bumble and Honey are coming for lunch. If you do the veg and the meat, I'll make the dessert. One of us will need to pop into the General Store to get a few bits and pieces as well," Mum went on. Even though there was nothing unusual about this conversation, it made Poppy feel sad. Her mum and dad talked like they were running a business together – it wasn't anything like the way Sally and Sol talked to each other. Maybe something was wrong. In fact, Poppy realized that it was very unusual for her parents to do anything together other than make plans and organize everyone's time.

After they had cleared up lunch Mum put the twins down for a nap and went off to her studio to start work on some hats.

"Poppy, why don't you go and play in your room while the twins are sleeping," suggested Dad. "We'll go down to the adventure playground in an hour or so."

"OK, Dad," agreed Poppy.

But instead of going to her room she ran upstairs – there was something she wanted to find.

Chapter Three

Poppy climbed the wobbly ladder that led into the attic and then turned on her torch. The attic was stuffed full with furniture, suitcases, old toys and boxes, all of which had labels on them. There was a box full of Christmas decorations, another containing curtains, one with dressing-up clothes and yet another labelled HALLOWEEN STUFF.

At first Poppy couldn't see what she was looking for, but when she moved some of the boxes out of the way, she soon found it. It was her parents' wedding box. It was incredibly beautiful – and big. The lid was decorated with silk flowers, pearly beads and sparkly crystals.

Poppy couldn't wait to look inside.

She carefully lifted the lid and shone the torch into the box. It was an absolute treasure trove. Mum's beautiful lace wedding dress was carefully folded with lavender tissue paper. Poppy gently unwrapped the dress and held it up against herself. She imagined how excited Mum must have felt on the morning of her wedding when she put it on, with Granny Mellow helping her. Mum must really miss her mum. Poppy certainly couldn't imagine life without *her* mum.

Then Poppy lifted another layer of tissue paper to reveal two bundles of letters and cards, one tied with lavender ribbon, the other with blue ribbon.

Wow! she thought. *These must be Mum and Dad's love letters. That's so romantic!*

The ones in the bundle tied with lavender ribbon were all addressed to "Sweet Lavender", while those tied with blue ribbon were to "Darling James". Poppy suddenly wondered why Mum and Dad never called each other by those names any more. She put the bundles down without reading the letters: even though she would have loved to, she knew that it would be wrong – these were private.

The final thing Poppy discovered in the box was a photograph of Mum and Dad on their honeymoon. As in their wedding photos, they both looked very happy, as if there was just the two of them in the whole world.

Poppy packed everything back up neatly and climbed down the ladder, realizing that it was probably time to go out with Dad and the twins.

She usually really enjoyed going to the adventure playground with Angel and Archie but today she was preoccupied. She couldn't stop thinking about all Mum and Dad's wedding stuff and how much they had seemed to love each other then, just like Sally and Sol; nowadays things were somehow different. The more Poppy thought about it, the more worried she became. She recalled family events – Dad was forever saying things like, "Don't tell Mum, she'll be cross with me!" or "It's up to Mum." She could tell from his voice that Dad respected Mum's ideas and opinions very much and wanted to please her. Poppy's dad was softer than her mum, but Mum was more organized – and *very* kind when you really needed her. Together they made a perfect team.

Poppy loved them both equally and she knew that they loved her and the twins very much as well. But she was very worried that they didn't love each other any more.

She hardly slept a wink that night thinking about her parents and was very pleased to see Honey at lunch the next day to talk over her

problems with her best friend. Together
they decided that they had to do something
– but what?

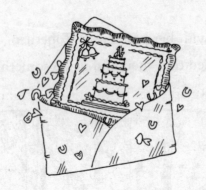

Chapter Four

The first Monday of the school holidays began with the excitement of Sally and Sol's wedding invitation arriving. This, coupled with Poppy's chat with Honey the day before, had made her feel a lot happier. Plus she was trying to come up with a plan to make everything better between her mum and dad – *and* Sally's special holiday craft classes were beginning that morning.

Poppy and her friends met for their class at the entrance to the Village Hall and were let in by Sally. They were all very excited: not only did they adore their craft sessions but they couldn't wait to hear more about Sally's wedding plans.

"Listen up, everyone," said Sally as they settled down at their places to start knitting their multi-coloured pencil cases. "I've got something to tell you. Sol and I have been talking about the details of our wedding. He has chosen his best man – which made me realize that I'd better think about my flower girls. I wondered whether to have one or two, but the problem was I couldn't decide *which* one or two I wanted

31

to ask – and that's because I want *all* of you to
be my flower girls!"

"Yippee!" cried the girls in unison.

"Wow! Thank you! I've never been a flower
girl before," said Sweetpea.

"What will we wear?" asked Abi.

"Ah, I knew someone would ask that!" Sally
smiled at them. "Well, each of you will have
a dress specially made for you by Saffron. I've
chosen a gorgeous fabric for the dresses – it's
printed with summer flowers. Lily Ann is going
to help with your hair – though you can wear

it in any style you like – and Holly Mallow is going to make charm bracelets for each of you."

Poppy was absolutely thrilled by this exciting news. She hadn't even dared to hope that she might be asked to be a flower girl. It would be so much fun to do it with all her friends from craft class too. She was very pleased indeed that she was going to be part of the main wedding party and get loads of attention. Poppy loved being at the centre of the action!

"Now, girls, calm down and let's get down to work," said Sally. "That's why we're here, after all. We will have to finish promptly today because I'm going on a date. Sol is taking me out for a yummy lunch in the City and then to the cinema."

When Poppy got home she was dying to tell Mum all about being asked to be a flower girl.

"Hi, Mum! Where are you?" she called out.

"I'm in my studio. Can you come and try on a hat for me while I stitch some flowers onto it, darling?"

"Course I can," said Poppy, who loved posing in front of Mum's fancy mirror.

"Guess what," she said to her mum as she stood modelling the hat. "I'm going to be a flower girl at the wedding!"

"Wow! That's great news, sweetheart!" said Mum. "Has Sally told you what sort of dresses you'll be wearing?"

"Well—" began Poppy excitedly, but she was interrupted by the crackle of the baby monitor: one of the twins was starting to cry.

"Back in a minute, darling!" said Mum.

But Poppy knew she wouldn't be back. Angel and Archie were so demanding; they always made Mum forget what she had been doing before. Poppy took off the hat and placed it carefully on Mum's workbench. Shortly after this, Dad returned from pricing a big gardening job, and before long he and Mum were discussing childcare arrangements, shopping lists and chores once again.

"Oh, I'm shattered," said Dad as he sat down at the kitchen table. "Any chance of a cup of tea?"

"*You're* shattered?" snapped Mum. "What about me?"

"I know, I know. It's harder work in the house than it is out of it. But I could do with a break," said Dad.

"Honestly, James. I can hardly keep my eyes open. I've got the kids, plus all these hats and—" Mum sounded as if she was at the end of her tether.

"I don't know why you agreed to do so many hats. You're always overworked and then you take it out on me," complained Dad.

"I take it out on you," Mum continued, "because I don't think you do your fair share around here."

Poppy hated it when Mum and Dad argued; it seemed to be happening way more often than it used to. She decided to go up to the attic.

At least she wouldn't be able to hear them from there. But their argument made her even more convinced that they didn't love each other any more. And then it came to her . . . What Mum and Dad needed was to go on a date – just like Sally and Sol – and then maybe they would fall in love all over again and forget their troubles.

Chapter Five

Poppy put her mind to organizing the date right away. She took out her notebook and wrote down a list of ideas.

Restaurant — they both like yummy food, but who would pay for it?

Theatre — would they like the same show? Very expensive!

Cinema — Dad likes action films and Mum likes weepies!

Shopping — makes them quarrel about money and how bad Mum is at making decisions. Maybe not.

Exhibition — maybe, if there was one about gardens, which they both love.

Sport — Dad would love this but Mum wouldn't.

When she looked at her list, she became more concerned than ever: it seemed as if Mum and Dad didn't even like doing the same things! Organizing this date was going to be more difficult than Poppy had anticipated so she decided to go up to the Sewing Shop and ask Saffron for some advice.

When she got there, Poppy explained to Saffron that she was planning a surprise for Mum and Dad's tenth wedding anniversary but that she was having trouble coming up with the perfect date.

"Oh, Poppy! You are a love, thinking about your mum and dad like that. What a good idea. I hope that when David and I have children they grow up to be as thoughtful as you are. Now, let me think . . . I reckon that if you're an exhausted mum and have to make lots of meals every day, then the best treat is probably to be cooked a delicious meal – all nicely presented with candles, wine and music."

"Good idea!" agreed Poppy. "Mum does get fed up with cooking all the time. She says she's running an All Day Café in our kitchen. I'll get to work on it now. Thanks, Saffron!"

Poppy returned home feeling much more positive than earlier and buzzing with ideas for the date. Now she just needed to sort out the details – and work out how to pay for it as she didn't have a lot of money left in her piggy bank.

. . .

Family life at Honeysuckle Cottage continued to be very hard at times. Poppy did her best to help but it didn't seem to do any good.

One morning she came into the kitchen to find Angel wearing the brand new silver sandals that she had saved up to buy from Saffron's shop. Poppy had been planning to wear them to the wedding. And worse still, Angel had drawn on them with felt pens.

"Angel! How could you do this?" shouted Poppy. "You ruin all my stuff. It was better before you were born!"

Angel began to cry. "Solly, Pop," she said over and over again. "Angel bad girl!"

"Poppy!" cried Mum. "Do you have to get so angry? Angel is only a baby."

"Lavender, I can understand why Poppy's upset — just look at those sandals," said Dad, feeling sorry for his elder daughter. "She saved up for those, remember?"

"Are we going to deal with discipline as a team or not, James?" snapped Mum.

Poppy flushed. "I'm sorry, Mum," she said. "I should never have lost my temper. I just loved those sandals."

"I know, darling, and Angel has been very naughty. I'm sorry as well," said Mum. "You have a lot to put up with, Poppy. It's just, well, you know, she doesn't mean to do these things – and maybe we can get the felt pen marks off them."

Dad tutted. "Honestly, Lavender. You need to be firm and keep a proper eye on the twins."

Mum exploded. "Why don't *you* keep an eye on them?"

Oh no, thought Poppy. Now she'd caused another fight between Mum and Dad. It was so easy to set them off.

Poppy knew that she had to get Mum and Dad out on this date before it was too late.

Chapter Six

The next day Poppy wandered over to the Lavender Valley Garden Centre, as she often did when she was at a loose end. Every time she'd been there lately, Sally was chatting to Sol about the wedding plans: it all sounded brilliant. Poppy had to admit that it was much more fun here than at her house.

"What do you think of this, Poppy?" Sally asked on one occasion. "Sol and I are going to Paris for our honeymoon!"

"That sounds amazing!" Poppy replied. She had heard that Paris was a very romantic city.

Sally and Sol were always laughing and

45

having fun together, plus they were so nice to Poppy. They seemed to have all the time in the world to listen to her.

As Poppy walked home, her heart was very heavy. Why couldn't Mum and Dad be more like Sally and Sol? Poppy was beginning to wish that *they* were her parents – they were so much more fun to be around and they never argued. She really hoped that the surprise she was planning for Mum and Dad would make them more like Sally and Sol.

Rather than go home right away, Poppy decided to visit Honey. She wanted to tell her about an idea she'd had to make her parents' date even more special.

"Hi, Honey," said Poppy. "Guess what? I've come up with another brilliant idea for Mum and Dad's special evening. Do you want to hear what it is?"

"Yes please," said Honey eagerly.

"As well as giving them a deeelicious meal under the oak tree in our garden, I'm going to make them a memory box to remind them how amazing their wedding day was and leave it under the tree for them to find."

"Wow! That's such a cool idea, Poppy."

"Thanks! I found their wedding guest list in

Mum's wedding box in the attic so I'm going to write a letter to everyone to see whether they've got anything connected with the wedding day that I can put in the memory box."

"But how will you get all the stuff without your parents seeing it?" asked Honey.

"Um, I hadn't got that far," confessed Poppy, suddenly feeling rather deflated.

"Maybe my granny will help," suggested Honey. "She loves surprises – I bet she's got some good stuff to put in the box too."

"That's a brilliant idea! Let's go and ask her now!" replied Poppy.

The girls raced over to Bumble Bee's Teashop and told Granny Bumble all about the plan.

"What a lovely idea. You are a thoughtful girl, Poppy. I'm sure I have a recipe for their wedding cake somewhere. We could put that in, couldn't we? It was a special one as they didn't want rich fruit or chocolate cake. They had rose-scented Victoria sponge cake with soft peppermint icing and butter-cream filling. Oh, it was absolutely

scrummy even if I do say so myself. I'll frame the recipe with a photo of the cake and give you that for your box, if you like."

"Oh, thank you, that would be lovely," Poppy said, delighted. "Actually, I wondered whether it would be OK if I ask everyone to leave the special box things here with you – that way Mum won't find out what I'm planning."

"No problem, love. Do you mind if I ask what is bringing all this on?" asked Granny Bumble. "Is it because of Sally's wedding?"

"Sort of. You see, it's nearly Mum and Dad's tenth anniversary and they don't act anything like Sally and Sol do, so I'm planning a surprise date for them," explained Poppy, not quite revealing the whole truth.

Granny Bumble chuckled. "That sounds wonderful. And what does that entail?" she asked.

"Well, Saffron thought that a yummy meal with wine and music would be the best thing. I'm going to set it out at the bottom of our garden under the big oak tree. Me and Honey

are going to decorate it like a fairyland so that
it is really magical – just like their wedding day,"
said Poppy proudly.

"It sounds like you've got it all worked out.
Aren't you girls clever?" said Granny Bumble.
"But who's going to look after the twins and
who will do the cooking?"

"I'm going to ask Saffron to babysit – she
loves taking care of Angel and Archie," replied
Poppy, "but I might need some help with the
cooking . . ."

"I'll help," offered Granny Bumble immediately. "I'm all in favour of exhausted parents having a good meal in peace. And I think I know all their favourite things. I'll make it so it's very easy to serve. They don't want us hovering around while they're having their anniversary dinner, now do they?"

"I suppose not," said Poppy, who *had* thought of spying from the tree house. However, she realized Granny Bumble was right. They needed complete privacy for their magical dinner date to work.

Chapter Seven

Poppy went home and wrote a letter to everyone on her parents' wedding guest list. Some were from college, which was where Mum and Dad first met. Her dad had been studying landscape gardening, and her mum had been in the year below him, studying hat making. Poppy imagined they'd had great fun back in those days when they were both students living in the big market town of Merrivale Marsh, which was about thirty miles from Honeypot Hill.

From the Offices of Princess Poppy Cotton
Honeysuckle Cottage
Honeypot Hill

Dear Friend,

It will soon be ten years since my mum
and dad, Lavender and James, got
married. I am going to make a
special memory box for them as a
surprise. I wonder if you could help
me by sending me any things you
have that are connected to their
wedding day. If you have
something, please leave it with
Granny Bumble at Bumble Bee's
Teashop, Honeypot Hill. This is a
SECRET! Please help me by being
very secretive.

Yours,
Princess Poppy

When Poppy had finished writing all the letters, she had a sandwich for lunch, then went round to call on Honey again.

"Will you help me deliver these letters?" she asked.

"Yeah, definitely. I'll just tell my granny," replied Honey.

"Good luck, girls!" called Granny Bumble as the two friends walked down towards the river. After posting a letter through Aunt Marigold's door they set off across the fields to deliver a letter to Saffron and another to Farmer and Mrs Meadowsweet. The next house on their list was the Turners' pretty cottage, which was in the grounds of Cornsilk Castle; then they headed back through the fields and over the bridge to give a letter to the Woodchesters at the Hedgerows Hotel. The last deliveries were to other local friends who lived on the outskirts of the village. Then they went past the post office and posted the remaining letters to the people who lived a little further afield.

"I can't wait to see what people bring to
Bumble Bee's Teashop!" exclaimed Poppy. "Now
I need to make a really beautiful box to put all
the stuff in. Will you help me?"

"I'd love to," replied Honey. "Let's go back to
your house now."

The girls found an old wooden box in the loft
and covered it with silky wedding fabric from
Mum's remnant box. Then they decorated it
with white ribbons, sequins and pearly beads.

"Let's use this wrapping paper to line the inside," suggested Poppy, who loved craft jobs like this.

"Good idea. It will look really pretty," agreed Honey.

"And when this is finished," announced Poppy, "we can get on with the rest of the plan – the best bit. We need to write the love letters. I can't do it because Mum and Dad will recognize my writing, so *you'll* have to."

"Oh, Poppy, I *can't* write love letters to your parents!" said Honey, who was really worried about getting caught.

"But, Honey, if you don't then the plan won't work and my mum and dad will carry on fighting all the time. Pleeease," begged Poppy.

Honey didn't want to let her best friend down but she was definitely not going to write love letters to Mr and Mrs Cotton. What if they found out? She'd be in such trouble with them *and* with Granny Bumble.

"I know," she said suddenly. "We could use my

new computer. If we type the letters they won't ever be able to tell who wrote them!"

"That's a brilliant idea, Honey!" said Poppy. "Let's go and do it now."

"Poppy, Honey," called Mum, "what are you girls up to?"

"Nothing," they replied in chorus.

"Well, you'd better both stop doing nothing. Poppy, it's time for supper. Honey, I'm sure Granny Bumble will be wondering where you've got to. I'll ring her and let her know you're on your way home."

Honey looked at Poppy. "Come round to my house tomorrow morning and we can do the letters then. My granny will be at the teashop so no one will know what we're doing," she suggested conspiratorially.

"Cool – see you then," replied Poppy. She couldn't wait.

The next day the girls sat in Honey's lovely yellow bedroom in front of her new computer and started to write the letters.

"A bit of mystery and romance is required here. It needs to be like Prince Charming writing to Cinderella," explained Poppy.

"I've never seen a love letter," confessed Honey. "I don't know what people put in them. I bet they're really yucky and lovey-dovey though. Did you read the love letters you found with your mum and dad's wedding stuff?"

"Ew, no," replied Poppy. "That would have been gross. I know what their pet names for each other were, though, so let's start with that."

Poppy dictated while Honey typed.

"There, that sounds good," said Poppy as she read what they had written. "Let's print them out!"

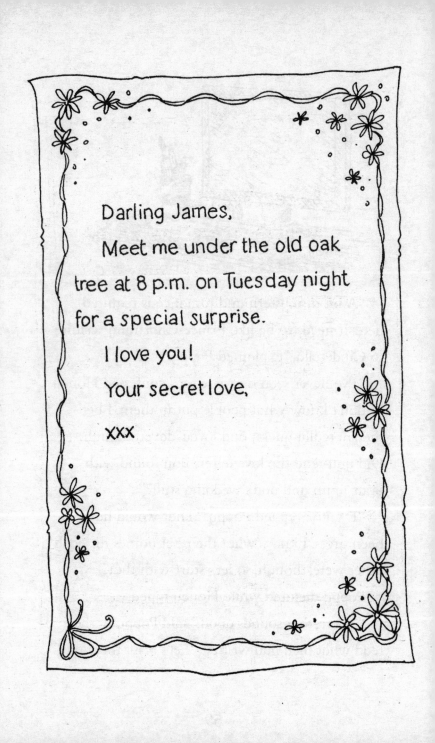

Darling James,

Meet me under the old oak

tree at 8 p.m. on Tuesday night

for a special surprise.

I love you!

Your secret love,

xxx

Sweet Lavender,

Meet me under the old oak tree at 8 p.m. on Tuesday night for a special surprise.

I love you!

Your secret love,

xxx

Poppy and Honey had it all organized.
Tomorrow they were going to decorate the
garden with fairy lights and set up a table with
candles and flowers. Just before Mum and Dad
were due to arrive Poppy planned to lay out the
delicious feast that Granny Bumble was making
for the occasion. The wedding box would be
placed near the table for her parents to discover
during dinner. Now all she had to do was make
sure they both received the love letters . . .

Chapter Eight

When Poppy got back, Mum was busy getting the twins ready to go to Grandpa's for the afternoon. He'd promised to look after them to give Mum a break for a few hours. This was the perfect time to plant the letters!

Poppy decided to leave the letter for Mum on the desk in her studio. Dad never went in there so he definitely wouldn't find it, and because Mum was working so hard at the moment she was in there all the time. The question of where to put the letter for Dad was more tricky. She thought about putting it in his golf bag, but then she remembered that he only played on Saturdays so he wouldn't find it in time. His trouser pocket was a possibility – but what if he decided to wear a different pair? Eventually Poppy decided to leave the letter in the drawer of his bedside table. Dad definitely looked in that every night because he kept his reading glasses and ear plugs there.

That should do it, thought Poppy when the letters were both in position.

Just then Honey arrived to pick her up for a dress fitting at Saffron's Sewing Shop. Mum seemed to be in a very good mood when the two friends set off, Poppy thought.

"Have fun, girls!" her mum called.

"Bye, Mum!" replied Poppy.

Poppy and Honey were both very excited about being measured for the dresses. They were still surprised and thrilled that they had been asked to be flower girls at all. It would be so much fun doing it with their friends.

"Right!" said Saffron as everyone assembled in her little shop. "Stand in a line alphabetically. We'll start with Abi at the front, then we'll have Helena, Honey, Lola, Mimosa, Poppy and Sweetpea. Now, I've made a chart for each of

you. I need your height, and then your waist, chest, arm and shoulder–to–waist measurements. And look, the fabric has arrived! Isn't it divine?"

Saffron held up a swatch of the soft flowery cotton.

"Wow! It looks like a summer garden," said Lola. "I love it."

"Me too!" said Poppy.

It made a nice change from shiny and sparkly materials – and it would be much more comfortable to wear on a warm summer's day as well.

Just as Saffron finished taking and noting down all the measurements, Lily Ann from the Beehive Beauty Salon arrived. It was time to talk about the girls' hairstyles for the wedding. They flicked through the glossy magazines Lily Ann had brought with her and chatted excitedly about the styles they liked.

"Sally wants you all to have a hairstyle that

suits you so I'm not going to try to make you all look the same. If we decide on the styles today, we can have a practice run nearer the time," explained Lily Ann.

After that Holly Mallow arrived to discuss the charm bracelets that Sally had promised her flower girls. She explained that each bracelet must reflect the personality or interests of the person who was wearing it.

"For example, if you like ponies, I can make a horseshoe charm for your bracelet."

As they were all chatting about the bracelets, how they wanted to wear their hair and whether or not they might grow it a bit before the wedding, Sally arrived at the little shop for a wedding dress fitting.

"Does that mean we get to see the dress?" asked Poppy.

"Well, I *might* let you have a peek," said Sally. "As long as you promise not to tell Sol anything about it!"

"Pinkie promise!" chorused the girls.

Ten minutes later Sally came out of the fitting room. The girls gasped. Sally hardly ever wore dresses because she was always working with plants and soil and water. This dress wasn't super fancy but it was just right and she looked amazing. It was creamy white with puff sleeves and a full skirt, complete with an overskirt.

"Sally, you look just like a princess!" exclaimed Poppy.

As the girls left the shop, Poppy's thoughts

turned back to her family. She couldn't wait
for Mum and Dad to find the secret notes;
she was sure that after the special surprise
dinner everything would be perfect again.
Poppy decided that instead of going straight
home, she would walk down to Bumble Bee's
with Honey to check that Granny Bumble had
everything ready for Mum and Dad's meal –
and to see if anyone had dropped by with
wedding day memorabilia.

Meanwhile at Honeysuckle Cottage, Mum had
almost finished a big tidy up of her study. Since
Grandpa was looking after the twins for the
afternoon, she had decided to do a few things
that she never managed to get done when they
were around.

"There, that feels better," she said to herself as
she opened the window to let in some fresh air.
It was nice to smell the summer flowers through
the open window, and the gentle breeze spread
the perfume throughout the house.

When she had finished in her study, Mum decided that she would have a lie down and read her book for a bit. But when she got to the bedroom she thought she might have a quick tidy up there before she settled down with her book. She always felt so much more relaxed when everything was in order.

As she put away clean clothes and dusted the surfaces, she noticed that the drawer of James's bedside table was slightly open. She pushed it

shut, and as she did so a small piece of paper fell out onto the floor. She picked it up to see what it was – and could hardly believe her eyes. It seemed to be a love letter to *her* husband!

What she didn't realize was that a similar letter for *her* had been gathered up with some old papers on her desk and thrown into the bin.

Chapter Nine

"Do you think your mum and dad will definitely find the love letters?" asked Honey as they walked to Bumble Bee's Teashop.

"Yeah, of course they will. It will be a perfect evening. And once they remember what it's like to go on dates, they can do fun stuff all the time. Come on, Honey, let's run. I'm dying to see if anything has been handed in for the memory box!"

"You seem very happy, Poppy!" said Granny Bumble as she set down a delicious strawberry cream tart for both the girls.

"We've just seen the fabric for our dresses and

it's lovely. Plus everything is all ready for Mum
and Dad's anniversary surprise!" replied Poppy.

"Jolly good," smiled Granny Bumble. "I've
got the meal under control, so tomorrow night,
when the table is set and the fairy lights are on,
just give me a shout and I'll deliver the food. Oh,
and just wait till you see all the pretty things that
have been delivered for your wedding box!"

She opened a
boutique bag and
revealed the wedding
day menu, supplied
by the chef at the
Hedgerows Hotel;
the order of service,
handed in by the
vicar; the invitation,
supplied by Aunt
Marigold; plus one of
Mum and Dad's thank-
you notes. There was also
a brilliant photograph

of their going-away car, which had been beautifully decorated by their friends from college.

"Wow! These things are great!" exclaimed Poppy. "Thank you for looking after everything for me."

When she had finished her snack and double checked with Granny Bumble that everything was set for the following night, Poppy walked back to Honeysuckle Cottage with the bag of memory box goodies. She went round the back and sneaked into her bedroom via the French windows so that she could stash the bag away without anyone seeing her. Then she went back out into the garden and re-entered the house by the kitchen door.

Poppy found Mum sitting at the kitchen table with a cup of tea in her hand. She seemed to be in a very strange mood – she looked like she had been crying.

"Hi, Mum. Are you OK?" asked Poppy.

"I'm fine, thanks, love. Just a bit tired. Why

don't you go and play in your room?"

"OK, see you later," replied Poppy. She was a bit worried about her mum but she was also pleased to have an opportunity to sort out the memory box without anyone disturbing her.

Poppy spent ages arranging the wedding things beautifully; when the wedding box was finished she hid it in her toy cupboard. She was so happy with the way everything was working out. She was convinced that the surprise date was going to be a huge success.

Half an hour later Poppy heard Grandpa and the twins come back so she raced into the kitchen to say hello. Grandpa stayed for a quick cup of tea and then went home to watch his favourite nature programme on the telly. Mum took charge of Angel and Archie and set about making supper. She was very quiet and Poppy thought she still looked miserable. Poppy couldn't think what might be wrong and Mum didn't seem to want to tell her – maybe she was just tired, like she had said.

While Mum was feeding the twins, Poppy heard Dad's car pull into the drive. A minute or two later he came in through the back door.

"Hi, everyone, I'm home!" he called. "The house looks great. You have been busy today, darling."

"Not as busy as you have obviously been lately!" stormed Mum.

Dad looked completely baffled.

"Poppy, can you keep an eye on the twins, darling?" asked Mum. "I need to talk to your father in the other room."

"OK," replied Poppy, wondering what was going on.

She knew that an argument was brewing, but what she didn't know was why. As she tried to entertain her baby brother and sister, Poppy could hear her parents talking in the next room.

"Lavender, what *are* you talking about?"

"Don't act so innocent, James!"

"Tell me what's going on, please," said Dad miserably.

"Explain this letter!" said Mum, thrusting the secret love note into his hands.

Poppy gasped – Mum had found the letter that was meant for Dad! It was all her fault that they were fighting. Things weren't going to plan at all. She had to do something.

Dad read the letter quickly. "I don't know anything about it. It must be a prank!"

"No one would play a joke like this," said Mum. "Have you been seeing someone behind my back? How *could* you, James?"

"Lavender, you have to trust me. I have no idea who wrote that letter. None whatsoever," Dad told her. "I would never let you down!"

Just then Poppy edged her way into the room.

"Mum, I think I might be able to explain . . ." she began.

"Poppy, go back to the kitchen and play with the twins, sweetie. Don't worry about anything," said Mum as soothingly as she could manage. "Supper will be ready soon."

"But—" Poppy tried again.

"No buts, darling," said Mum. "This is between me and your dad."

79

She wanted to believe her husband but she had nagging doubts in her mind. "Let's just have supper and try to get through this," she said.

Poppy was distraught. It looked like her carefully thought out surprise would have to be cancelled. What a disaster – and it was all her fault.

After a miserable and silent supper Poppy ran over to Honeypot Cottage to see Honey and Granny Bumble.

Chapter Ten

Poppy burst into the cosy cottage and found
her friend and Granny Bumble in the kitchen
clearing up supper.

"Hello, love!" said Granny Bumble. "What
brings you over here again?"

Poppy explained what had happened and that
Mum and Dad's surprise dinner would have to
be cancelled. Then she then started sobbing.

"Oh dear!" Granny Bumble gave her a hug.
"You are in a pickle. You know, the best thing
to do is tell your parents what you've done.

They might be cross to start off with but they won't be for long, I promise you."

"I've tried," said Poppy in between sobs, "but they won't listen to me!"

"Well, keep trying, dear. Everything will work out in the end. You mark my words," Granny Bumble told her.

That night, when Mum came in to kiss Poppy goodnight and tuck her in, she was looking very tired and sad and Poppy knew that if she tried to explain things, Mum would just tell her to

stop. When Mum had gone Poppy tossed her
favourite fairytale book into the back of her toy
cupboard. After everything that had happened
she was beginning to think that fairytales
were silly.

Poppy couldn't stop worrying that her mum
and dad didn't love each other any more – and
that she had made things worse with her stupid
date idea. Still, there was a wedding to look
forward to, she told herself. Poppy loved what
she was wearing and thought that Sally and
Sol's plans sounded wonderful, but she could not
summon up her usual enthusiasm. Worst of all,
Mum and Dad were so busy that despite all her
efforts Poppy still hadn't managed to explain the
mix-up with the love letter. Things between her
parents were very frosty indeed.

One night not long before the wedding, when Mum was tucking Poppy in, she noticed that the fairytale book was missing.

"What happened to the fairy stories Grandpa gave to you?" she asked.

"I don't believe in fairy tales any more," said Poppy sadly.

"Oh, Poppy!" said Mum. "Don't be so silly. Fairy tales are wonderful – you're much too young to stop believing in them. *I* still believe! Night, night, darling! Sleep tight."

Now that Poppy had got into this sad mood, she was always noticing how happy other people's parents were – so much happier than her own – and it made her worry even more. It seemed to her that no one else's parents squabbled. She paid special attention when she was at Peppermint Pond with Grandpa and the twins. Abi's mum and dad were laughing and holding hands as they walked their new Dalmatian puppy. On the way back she saw Saffron and David through the window of

the Hedgerows Hotel.
They were chatting
and laughing and
holding hands over a
meal. As she walked
along the river bank
she saw Sweetpea's
mum and dad out
cycling. They were
having a race and were
giggling and calling
out to one another.

Back at
Honeysuckle Cottage
Poppy heard Mum and
Grandpa chatting over
a cup of tea while she
played with the twins
in the sitting room.

"She's not herself,
Lavender," said
Grandpa. "I don't

know what's up, but there's definitely something bothering her. She hardly spoke at all while we were out – and that's very unlike the Princess Poppy I know!"

"Everything's fine," said Mum. "I've just taken on too much work for the wedding, that's all, Dad, and I think Poppy's feeling a bit left out. Although the other night she did say she didn't believe in fairy stories any more. I never thought I'd see the day . . . But I'm sure it's just a phase."

"Well, you know best, but we don't want our princess to stop believing in fairy tales for ever, do we?" said Grandpa.

Poppy thought about what Grandpa had said. She remembered that there were always lots of problems in all her fairy stories, but that true love conquered all in the end. Maybe things would work out OK after all – she just needed a new plan.

That night Poppy got the fairytale book out of her cupboard and read through it for ideas.

*Hmmm. Snow White . . . Sleeping Beauty . . .
Cinderella – it's always the prince who rescues the
princess. Really it's up to Dad to be the hero*, thought
Poppy. *But maybe he needs a little help. I know what!
I'll order some flowers to be delivered. Mum's favourites
– white lilies!*

The next day Poppy tipped her pennies out of
her piggy bank into her purse and went to ask
Sally to make a special delivery to Honeysuckle
Cottage.

"No problem, Poppy. What shall I put on the
card?" asked Sally.

"Just write *To my Sweet Lavender!*" replied
Poppy.

Sally smiled. "Right-o!"

Back at the cottage Poppy waited impatiently for the delivery. She was sure that this would fix everything. Finally the flowers arrived and Mum was thrilled.

"Oh, my favourites!" she exclaimed. "Maybe James is trying to say sorry!"

When Dad came through the front door after work Mum ran to meet him.

"Thank you for the flowers, darling!" she said.

"What flowers?" asked Dad.

"Very funny, James! The white lilies, of course!"

Dad's face was a picture of confusion. "Let me see the card, Lavender!"

Dad took the card and quickly read it. "Who else calls you Sweet Lavender?" he asked. "You must have an admirer! I certainly didn't send these ..."

Now *Dad* was jealous!

"First of all I discover a love letter you know nothing about and now I get flowers you know nothing about! What *is* going on?" said Mum.

Chapter Eleven

Poppy realized that yet again she had done more harm than good. She simply didn't know what to do to make things better.

She went to the dress fittings and the church rehearsal the day before the wedding, but she could no longer feel her princess sparkle inside. Honey could see that her friend was not her usual self and tried to reassure her that everything was going to be fine. Plus she wanted to have fun with Poppy on the wedding day.

Poppy smiled. Thank goodness she had Honey to comfort her.

When she got home Mum was in a really

good mood because the last hat had been picked up. It was for Mrs Meadowsweet and she was delighted with it.

"How was the rehearsal, darling?" asked Mum.

"Oh, it was OK," replied Poppy quietly. "I'm really tired though. I'm going to have a bath and go to bed early."

"Very sensible, sweetheart. Tomorrow's a big day. We'll come and tuck you in when you're ready."

Poppy had a lovely bubble bath, then put on her rosebud pyjamas. As she was drying her hair, Mum and Dad said goodnight to the twins, and sat down to plan the wedding day for the Cotton family.

"I'm really worried about Poppy," said Mum, putting aside their problems.

"Me too!" agreed Dad. "She's awfully quiet considering there's a wedding tomorrow and fancy frocks to enjoy."

"Let's go and tuck her in and have a chat," said Mum.

Mum and Dad tiptoed into Poppy's room. She was sitting at her dressing table, sorting through a beautiful satin box.

"What's that, darling?" asked Mum.

"Nothing," said Poppy, putting the lid on the box.

"Come on, darling. No secrets!"

"Um, well, the thing is . . . actually, I have kept a few secrets lately," confessed Poppy as she got under her bedclothes.

"Come on, you know you can tell us anything," said Dad. "And perhaps you'll even show us what's in that pretty box!"

"The thing is," began Poppy, "I'm worried that you two don't love each other any more. Sally and Sol are so happy and romantic and it made me notice how you never do anything fun together; you've been fighting loads recently too. I wanted to make things better so I sent the love notes using Honey's new computer, but Mum's letter got lost. You were supposed to have a lovely meal under the oak tree at the bottom of the garden. But I had to cancel it. And then I arranged for the flowers to be sent to Mum, but that was a mistake too. And no one would listen to me when I tried to explain!" she finished.

Mum and Dad didn't know whether to laugh or cry!

"Oh, Poppy!" laughed Mum. "I feel so much better now! And to think that your dad and I were suspicious of each other!"

"I tried to tell you!" said Poppy.

Dad started to laugh. "Poor darling! You shouldn't have to worry about us. We're just as happy as ever. But there is one brilliant

thing to come out of what you've done," he
told her.

"What?" asked Poppy.

"You made Mum and me so jealous that
we've realized we are just as crazy about each
other as ever!"

Poppy laughed and Mum and Dad joined in.
She hadn't seen them this happy for ages.

"Can we see what's in the box now?" asked
her mum.

Poppy handed them the beautiful memory
box.

"Oh, James! Look at this!" said Mum.

They looked at all
the wonderful things and
recalled the happy day.

"Poppy, you are
such a thoughtful girl.
Remember the cake
– oh, and look at the
car. I'd forgotten about
that," said Mum.

Poppy drifted off into a happy sleep as Mum and Dad talked about their wonderful day ten years before.

The next morning she woke up with a different feeling inside her. She was her usual happy self again. She knew that Mum and Dad would still squabble sometimes, but now it wouldn't worry her. She got ready early and waited patiently while the rest of the family dressed.

"Will we *ever* get out of here on time?" said Grandpa to Poppy as they waited for Mum to get ready.

"Grandpa, the princess can take as long as she likes," said Poppy.

"Ah! Mum is the princess, is she?" asked Grandpa.

Poppy nodded. "And Dad is Prince Charming!"

"What a fuss weddings are!" moaned Dad as he came into the room. "I've only got one

cufflink and one shoe! And I can't find
my wallet!"

Poppy and Grandpa laughed.

"Here's your wallet, Dad!" said Poppy.

As she passed it to him, a photo of Mum
taken on their wedding day fell out of
it. She bent down and
picked it up.

"Thanks, Poppy!"
said Dad. "I love that
photo – Mum looks so
beautiful, doesn't she?"

Just then Mum
appeared, looking
stunning in a pale pink
dress with a matching rose hat.

"You're just as lovely as you were on our
wedding day!" Dad told her.

"Come on, you two!" said Poppy. "There's
no time for romance at the moment!"

Mum and Dad laughed.

The whole family enjoyed the wedding.
Poppy saw Mum and Dad holding hands and
smiling at each other when the vows were being
taken; they were even giggling and whispering
to each other – just like Sally and Sol did all
the time. After the ceremony Dad and Poppy
went off to the marquee to dance.

"Dad, your disco dancing is rubbish!"
said Poppy.

"I know," agreed Dad. "You'll have to show me how to do it, Poppy. In fact, I can learn a lot from you, darling. From now on, Mum and I are going to have a night out together every month. We have realized how important it is to show love as well as feel it – all thanks to our special princess."

Poppy smiled and got on with her next important job – teaching Dad to disco dance – confident that they would all live happily ever after!

THE END

THE END

Read a chapter from
Princess Poppy's next adventure,

The Hidden Jewels . . .

Princess Poppy
The Hidden Jewels

Chapter One

Honey flew down Poppy's front path like
a graceful fairy and ran into Honeysuckle
Cottage.

"Poppy!" she called breathlessly. "Where
are you? I've got some amazing news!"

Poppy appeared from her bedroom,
where she had been making a necklace.
"Hi, Honey! What is it?" she asked.

"Well," began Honey, "my mum and dad
are coming next week and they're going to
stay for a whole month."

Poppy was delighted for her best friend.

"Wow, Honey. That's so cool. I can't wait either. Your mum and dad are the best fun!"

Honey beamed from ear to ear. "I'm going to write the date on my calendar and tick off the days," she declared. "I can hardly wait!"

Honey spent the next week preparing everything for her parents' arrival. Together with Granny Bumble she spring-cleaned the cottage from top to bottom. Granny Bumble did lots of baking and even had her hair specially set by Lily Ann Peach at the Beehive Beauty Salon. Then the two of them got the spare bedroom ready, making up the bed with crisp white sheets and a cosy patchwork quilt. As a

finishing touch they picked
some pretty flowers in the
garden, arranged them in
a vase and put them on the
dressing table. Honey's mum
absolutely adored flowers.

After what seemed like an age the big day
finally arrived. The night before her parents
were due, Honey was in such a state of
excitement that she hardly slept a wink.
But now that the day had come at long
last, nothing else mattered. Honey simply
couldn't wait to see them. Every time she
heard a car drive through the village she
dashed outside in the hope that it was them,
even though she knew they weren't due until
the afternoon. At last, while Granny Bumble
was preparing tea, Honey heard another
car. This time she was sure it was her mum
and dad.

"Look, Granny, it's them!" she squealed as
she dashed out of the front door, down the

garden path and through the gate so that she could greet her parents at the roadside.

Honey fell into her mother's arms.

"Honey, darling, you look wonderful! And you've grown so much – you'll be as tall as me soon," gasped her mum.

"I've missed you, Mum," she said.

Before she really knew what was happening, Honey found herself being scooped up in a huge bear hug by her dad. Then he twirled her in the air until she was dizzy – just like he always did.

"And how's my fairy princess?" he asked. "Pretty as ever, I see."

Just then Granny Bumble came out of the cottage, smoothing down her apron, pushing an unruly curl behind her ear and smiling broadly. She was absolutely thrilled to see her son and daughter-in-law, and although she hadn't admitted it to Honey, she'd been so excited she hadn't slept a wink the night before either!

"Welcome! How are you? You must be exhausted after your flight. Come in and have some tea and then we can unpack the car," she said.

The Bumble family spent a relaxed evening together, catching up on everything they'd been doing since they last saw each other. Before long it was as if Honey's mum and dad had never been away.

The next day after school, Honey's parents, Daniel and Jasmine, were waiting for Honey and Poppy outside Rosehip School in their fancy hire car.

"Hi, girls! We're going on a mystery tour!" explained Daniel. "Poppy, I've spoken to your mum and she says it's OK for you come too!"

"Yippee!" cried Honey as she and Poppy climbed into the back seat.

As soon as their seat belts were fastened, the car sped off out of Honeypot Hill.

Daniel took lots of back lanes so that
Honey and Poppy had no idea where they
would end up. After a while they saw the
sea ahead, and the girls realized they were
driving towards Camomile Cove. Daniel
parked the car near the harbour and they
all got out and decided to have a wander
around the town. Poppy and Honey were
delighted to have a chance to show off
their favourite shops, Ned's Saddlers and
Bijou. They were even more delighted when
Honey's mum bought each of them a pretty
new handbag.

"And now for another surprise!" said Honey's dad as he led them back towards the harbour. "I've booked a boat ride across the bay."

"Yippee!" chorused Poppy and Honey.

"Can we have ice-cream sundaes in the Lighthouse Café afterwards?" asked Honey.

"Of course you can, sweetheart," smiled Jasmine, thrilled that their first outing was proving to be such a success.

For the first few days of the Bumbles' visit it was like one big holiday, even though it was still term time. Poppy and Honey were having so much fun. They went to a huge toy store in the city, dined in lots of lovely restaurants, played tennis and rounders, and had lots of get-togethers with other friends in the village. But after a week of fun Honey's dad began to feel rather restless. He was used to his phone ringing constantly and rushing from one meeting to another. He simply wasn't good at not working.

One night, after her mum had put her to bed, Honey was thinking what a wonderful time she was having with her parents and imagining all the fun they would have together during the rest of their stay. She was feeling utterly content – until she overheard her parents talking in their room, which was right next to hers. Suddenly her happy little bubble burst.

Princess Poppy
A True Princess

Poppy is feeling very sorry for herself.
She is convinced that everyone likes her
best friend Honey more than they like
her and that they think she is prettier too!
Poor Poppy doesn't even believe that
she is a true princess any more!

Princess Poppy
Ballet Dreams

Poppy and Honey are thrilled when
Madame Angelwing starts extra ballet
classes. At first, Poppy loves them, but she
soon feels that ballet is taking over her life.
When Honey decides to stick with
the classes and no longer has any time
for her best friend, Poppy feels very sad.

www.princesspoppy.com

Princess Poppy
The Fashion Princess

Poppy and Saffron are at New York Fashion
Week. They've got an action-packed
itinerary, including fashion shows and
a city tour. But when Poppy finds the
supermodel Tallulah Melage sobbing
in a corner, she realizes that there's
a darker side to all the glitz.

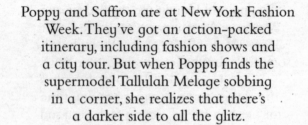

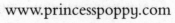

www.princesspoppy.com

Princess Poppy
Haunted Holiday

Poppy and Honey are going to France
to stay in an enormous castle and they
can't wait. It's the first time Poppy's
ever been abroad or stayed in a castle.
But as soon as they arrive,
strange things start happening . . .

Princess Poppy
Pony Club Princess

Poppy is taking part in a Pony Club
competition with her cousin Daisy. They've
both been practising like mad and they
absolutely can't wait. But before long
a whole series of things start to go
wrong and it looks like Poppy might
not be able to compete after all.